K. I. Campbell

**Mairi of Callaird**

A west Highland Tale

K. I. Campbell

**Mairi of Callaird**
*A west Highland Tale*

ISBN/EAN: 9783337137786

Printed in Europe, USA, Canada, Australia, Japan

Cover: Foto ©Andreas Hilbeck / pixelio.de

More available books at **www.hansebooks.com**

# MAIRI OF CALLAIRD.

## A WEST HIGHLAND TALE,

TRANSLATED FROM THE GÆLIC AS ORALLY COLLECTED.

VERSIFIED: AND DEDICATED TO

## MAC CAILEIN MOR,

*DUKE OF ARGYLL,*

BY A KINSWOMAN.

*K. I. C., June,* 1878.

# INTRODUCTION.

THE following is a metrical English version of part of a local Gælic tradition, which was orally collected in Glencoe and about Lochawe. Soon after the popular tales of the West Highlands were published in 1860-62, one of the peasant collectors, a woodman at Rosneath, was employed to gather traditional county history and family legends for the Duke of Argyll. John Dewar collected orally from people of his own class, who still remember a great abundance of traditions of all kinds. He wrote in Gælic. His manuscripts were read, and sorted, and bound in seven large volumes, which are preserved in the library at Inveraray Castle. They escaped the fire in October, 1877.

In August, 1877, a volume was taken on board of a yacht, and stories were translated from it during a cruise amongst the Islands. Part of one of these translations has now been versified. The Gælic prose version, as orally collected and put together by the collector, begins at page 200, Vol. II. of Dewar's manuscript, and is thus headed :

"A Tale about Mary of Callaird, or Mary Cameron, and MacDhonachaidh, of Inveràth."

The original tells how Glencoe was occupied at first, and gives many legends about the lands on both sides of Loch Leven. "Duncan's son" is the patronymic of the head of an old Campbell family, whose ancestor in the main stem was Duncan, one of the Black Knights of Lochawe. The present MacDhonachaidh, Campbell of Inveràth, according to tradition, is the 22nd of this branch tribe of Campbells. The date of the story is fixed about 1645, by mention of the battle of Inverlochy, at which the hero of the tale was slain. It is true that one of the family of Inveràth married a lady of the Callaird family, and one of them fell at Inverlochy.

A plague visited Glasgow in 1646. The members of the University then removed to Irvine (Sketches of Early Scotch History : Innes, Edinburgh, 1861, page 420). In 1625 a great mortality prevailed in London. The Great Plague of London was in 1665. In this story a plague ship is said to have come from Sweden, or, according to others, from Italy, with dye stuffs and linens. In Southern Norway it is said that whole districts were depopulated about this time by the Plague. Plagues also raged in France, Sardinia, and Italy between 1632 and 1656. In the Highlands and Islands of Scotland, sites of farms and villages are commonly shewn which were abandoned, according to local tradition during a great sickness, which is still called "the Black Death." A plague so called, raged in Italy in 1340, which spread through Europe and to Great Britain and Ireland. The name has been remembered. The story of the plague at Callaird House, shortly before the battle of Inverlochy, fought 1645, is thus supported by general history. About the time the plague was rife.

In September, 1877, a herdsman, who had come down from the Black Mount with cattle to Baile Chaolais, there met the writer by chance. He knew all the chief incidents in the story, and pointed to many of the places named in it, .which are within sight of the ferry. An ordnance map and memory enabled the translator and the lady who composed the following metrical version of part of the translation, to identify and describe the localities.

In 1876 a version of this oral popular history was printed for the second time. It is called on the title page, "A Highland Story. Incidents relating to the Massacre of Glencoe and the Plague at Callart House: by John Cameron, Bard to the Ossianic Society. Second Edition. Glasgow: William Gilchrist, Printer, 64, Howard Street, 1876." Dewar's version is fuller; he consulted more peasant authorities, and got more incidents. The Bard has framed his word pictures. He gives his own metrical Gælic version of the tradition, which was orally collected by Dewar about 1865, and was also told to the writer by a herd in September, 1877. The Gælic poet imitates MacPherson's Ossian ; his "Arguments" are in English. In notes at page 31, &c., he gives, in English, an outline of the adventures of several generations of the Callaird family, as remembered traditionally in the district.

Dewar carries the family history down to the tragic death of Mary. She and her party were overwhelmed by the fall of a cliff, under which they had taken shelter during a thunderstorm, while on their way to Islay with her second husband, the Prior of Ardchattan. She married him after her first husband was slain at Inverlochy. Some of her Gælic songs are still remembered and much admired.

A story so widely known to the people of a large district, probably is true in the main. The manner of telling it belongs to narrators, and to Bards who turn prose into verse and adorn it. The foundation is fact.

This, then, is the history of the preservation of a popular tradition of the West Highlands, of which the following is a metrical version. It illustrates the growth of legends, and of compositions founded upon them.

J. F. CAMPBELL,
NIDDRY LODGE, KENSINGTON,
*June*, 1878.                                          LONDON, W.

# MAIRI OF CALLAIRD.

—:o:—

In days gone by, when ruder was the land,
And feudal chiefs their followers might command,
While, ready in the fray to win or fall,
Each faithful clansman answered to the call,
Fierce jealousies kept men apart, more wide
Than loch and hill did neighbouring glens divide,
And wrong inherited made worse that wrong
As with avenging steel it armed the strong.
Yet were those times not altogether dark,
Bright through the gloom shot forth th' electric spark
Of generous thought, that would ennoble youth,
Where in the heart breathed chivalry and truth;
And stirred thereby, oft daring deeds were done
Which sweet success and long remembrance won.

In favoured spots more peaceful than the rest,
With homely wealth th' inhabitants were blest ;
There simple worth and innocence abode,
And through such channels acts of kindness flowed
To those whom fortune with a niggard hand
Had passed, or gifted with a shivered wand.
Of these past days, relate we now a tale
Which sympathy to win can scarcely fail.


On Caledonia's sea-indented shore,
Rich in that wild traditionary lore
Of which each glen and inlet record bears:
Where Leven's water gentle aspect wears ;
There lived a man of Cameron race and name,
Which race, tho' later proudly known to fame,
Then long, as was the wont of freeborn Celt,
In turbulent obscurity had dwelt.
This lochlet takes its narrow eastward way
From Linnhe's tidal waves which further stray,

And in the midst of lofty hills that rise
To mountain grandeur there embosomed lies.
Its western end by jutting point of land
Is narrowed still; this entrance to command
Needs but slight wardenship; the point outside,
The waters roll in lengthening fuller tide,
Till reaching far past shore and island lee,
They mingle in the depths of open sea.
On Leven's northern side, in fair array,
The house and spreading lands of Callaird lay;
Sheltering the turret-roof Maam-Callaird rose
In gentle slope, where still the heather grows;
Thence o'er the surface south and eastward gaze,
And hills on hills behold, now part in haze,
Or hid by changing clouds that deeper shade
The dark rich hues by fir and heather made,
Which clothe the sloping sides—now standing forth
In clear relief—the giants of our north;
Their stony tops, in cold and glittering sheen
Contrasting with the glens that lie between.

And when the sinking sun casts roseate tint
Upon the nearer peaks and distant glint,
When creeping shadows deep and deeper grow,
As evening mists enwrap the vales below ;
When with departing day all Nature sinks
To silent rest, from which guilt only shrinks ;
When all is hushed in sweet refreshing sleep,
And few save bat and owlet vigil keep ;
Then upward still, the vision seeks for light
And finds it in the starry shimmer bright,
Where glitter worlds unnumbered and unknown ;
Their varying path by distant radiance shown.
What scene more glorious can the eye demand
From Nature, stern, cold, beautiful and grand.
Still Southward look, and closer survey take
Where opes a glen whose name will ever make
The mirthful shudder and the grave more grave, —
For it proclaims how fiend-like can behave
Destroying man unto his fellow-man,
When thirst of blood doth with such fury fan

His fiery wrath, that he will basely deign
His victor's shield with treachery to stain.
Who has not heard that direful tale of woe,
The deeds there done—the terrors of Glencoe ?
And though such deeds, approved in bygone days,
Have been but rarely known as Britons' ways,
Yet cruelties and wars in every clime
Lie darkly brooding in the womb of time ;
And sad it is for those doomed spots of earth
That feel the throes, and own their murderous birth.
But with our story crime has nought to do,
And we would fain unwind its silver clue.


The laird of Callaird had a daughter fair ;
So fair and pure that with her might compare
But few of earth's more known and lovely ones
Born to subdue, and bless (or curse) her sons.
Among her kindred there the maid was seen
Gracious in sweet simplicity of mien.

Her smile was gentle as her voice was kind,
No falseness lurked her eye's calm glance behind;
It met you with a quiet look and frank,
Though admiration's gaze the eyelids sank
Reprovingly before; those dark-fringed lids
Veiled orbs of clearest blue from vulgar stare
Of stranger rude ; thus modesty forbids
Approach, and teaches folly to forbear.
But why describe the beauties of her face,
Or seek attraction's subtle power to trace ?
It is not always in the perfect line
Of features rare we can that power define;
We see it in the sparkling speaking eye,
The rising blush, the look of softness shy ;
We hear it in the silvery laugh, not loud
But sweetly clear, that vibrates thro' the crowd;
The tender tones that linger on the ear
With sympathetic force, though none be near ;
We feel it in the restless wish to win
The kindly smile, and live its sway within ;

The longing to be ever at the side,
And there in ecstasy of secret pride,
While others fret at darkly gathering sky,
At pattering rain and tempest raging high,—
Impatient how their idle hours to fill—
To feel for us that it is sunshine still :
And in this sweet bewilderment we dream,
Unconscious of the passing of life's stream,
Till comes some trifling act disturbing much,
A word, a look, and with the magic touch,
A thought of joy, it may be from above—
We wake to know that what we feel is love.
Thus steals into the heart the master-power
That subjugates the strong and rules the hour ;
And if rebellion break the bondage sweet,
And coward falsehood turn with flying feet,
No after source of pleasure can restore
The first bright spell that can be felt no more.
Though smiles and wit and laughter may abound,
In conscience pricked a Nemesis is found.

But fickleness or folly could not mate
With Callaird's daughter, nor becloud her fate,
For she was one impetuous youth t' inspire
With feelings that could never change or tire.
Like as her native fir amid the grove
Rears its tall shaft all other trees above,
So Mairi showed 'mong damsels fair of face,
Alone in slender stateliness and grace;
And with a form the eye would fain pursue,
Her mind was noble and her heart was true;
So good, so kind, and pitiful withal,
Her ear ne'er turned from misery's plaintive call;
And liberal to a fault, so all might live,
She would with both hands ever freely give.
The poor would seek her, and her nimble feet
Ne'er tarried sorrow helpfully to meet.
Thus softly moving in her mountain home,
Where city ways and pleasures were unknown
And books were scarce, except the holy tome,—
In works of kindliness her years had grown.

There still unto the Gael her name is dear,
Still to her story lends he willing ear,
Nor in his memory doth its interest fade,
So well was loved that gentle Cameron maid.


There came a time of want and sore distress,
When aye the porridge bowl held less and less,
And weak and weaker grew the infant wail
Till hushed in death's kind arms were pillowed pale
Those whom the sorrowing heart and sinking frame
Would view with eyes all lustreless and dim,
Content that ghastly power the loved should claim,
If but the piteous cry, the writhing limb
Could only so be stilled, and suffering o'er.
Then would the poor draw nigh the rich man's door
For meal to beg or borrow from his store.
From this full store, the elder daughter's charge,
'Twas Mairi's wont to give in measure large.
Dispensing thus the all too-precious grain,
When seed-time came, but little did remain.

" How is it, girl ? of seed there's not enough ? "
And in his wrath the laird spoke loud and rough.
" Dear father, I but gave what thou could'st spare.
"E'en were thy stackyard altogether bare,
" I knew that thou hadst money and could'st buy
" If need there were—the poor could only die.
" In their extremity I pitied them—
" Oh do not this as an offence condemn."
" Weak, foolish girl, soon would'st thou waste my gold,
" For ways like thine, no purse enough could hold.
" Begone, and leave my house, and take thy way
" The cold world through—and do as best thou may.
" See then if others be as kind to thee
" As thou hast been to them—it scarce will be.
" The world is stern, and proving it alone
" Will teach its hardening truths—now be thou gone.
" Nay, tears are useless—I will have it so."
And Mairi heard, and weeping turned to go.
She knew the hasty temper ne'er could brook
Reply, yet lingered for relenting look.

None came her soft imploring glance to meet,
So with a pang at heart that faster beat,
Obedient to his word, she left him there.
She passed the little sister on the stair,
Who marked the falling tear, but with the awe
Which childhood feels at sight of elders' grief,
No question asked—stern was parental law
Within that household, where still reigned belief
In right unchallenged of domestic rule.
The wrath so quickly roused, as soon might cool
If unopposed; but ill indeed it fared
With those who in his anger crossed the laird.
E'en she, the trusted, most indulged of all
Must bear reproaches, bitter past recall.
There was no help—the brothers were afield;
And were they not, small comfort could they yield.
Her plaid she donned, allowing first short space
To check th' emotion showing in her face,
Then on the doorstep met again the child;
This time with look that would not be repelled,

And violets in the offering hand upheld.
Affection's tribute sorrow's course beguiled ;
She kissed the giver, and the curly head
Caressed—" I to Lundavra go," she said,
And forthwith o'er the garden grass-walk sped.


Maam-Callaird's Pass along her steps she bent,
And wounded pride unto them firmness lent,
Altho' it flushed her cheek and dimmed her eye.
The breeze was keen, and dull and grey the sky
In lowering clouds hung coldly overhead,
And the fair scene with dreariness o'erspread.
Yet keener came the blast, as, upward still
Her way pursuing by the Spring-clad hill
Where, later, mountain berries would abound,
She shivering wrapped more close her plaid around.
What form is this that moves with step so slow ?
" Oh, lady dear, some help on me bestow,

" For I am weak and cold, and scarce do find
" My strength suffice to battle with this wind."
" Poor wanderer, to an empty hand dost come,
" For, penniless, I'm banished from my home.
" My father sends me thence in sore disgrace
" Nor know I when again I'll see his face."
" Yet, lady, comfort thee—thy heart if pure,
" And spotless if thy conscience—time will cure
" All lesser evils; there is One above
" Who cares for all with more than mortal love;
" For thee, for me—Who tempereth the wind
" To the shorn lamb.  Cast then thy grief behind
" And forward look.  Forgive my words thus bold
" Nor let them in thine ear disfavour hold."
" Good Mother, thou hast done a kindly part
" And I will lay thy precept well to heart.
" I would I better guerdon could command
" Than gentle speech, that filleth not the hand:
" Yet stay, the little that I have I'll share
" With thee in all goodwill," and promptly there

Her plaid upon the ground the damsel spread,
Then straightway cut its length in twain, and said
" Take thou the half, 'twill shield thee from the blast."
" Now blessings on thee, sweet and generous maid,
" For sharing thus thy warm and goodly plaid;
" But thou who givest richer blessing hast
" Than I who take.  I, too, would something give,
" So may this hour long in thy memory live.
" See here this seeming nut with circling band
" Of darker brown—clear-marked by Nature's hand.
" 'Tis called a fairy egg, and may be so,
" For how or whence it cometh none yet know.
" At times upon this western outer shore
" Where break the billows in their ceaseless roar,
" Bearing strange burdens o'er th' unfathomed deep,
" Do men such jetsam joy to find and keep.
" The weak and foolish think they are a charm
" To bring good fortune, and protect from harm;
" To guard from pestilence, from sinking prow,
" To keep the lover faithful to his vow;

" But thy firm heart, and thy yet firmer mind,
" Will in these fancies naught but folly find :
" For thee the blessing breathed by grateful age
" A hundredfold will more thy cares assuage,
" And the remembrance dear of kindness done
" Will smoothe its roughness as thy course is run.
" Thy soul in strength and calmness will await
" Futurity, and bearing, conquer fate.
" Take then this humble gift, and with it take
" My heart's best thanks, that most its value make.
" Thy way is onward—up Life's mountain path,
" Mine to the vale that rest and shelter hath.
" Farewell." " May peace be with you, I must on,
" And go the happier for thy benison."
And with the lighter step of youth and hope
The maiden trod the long and toilsome slope.


Before her now, in near uprising might,
Mullach na Coirean rears his stony height,

And distant more, dark rolling clouds between,
Ben Nevis shows his crest of snowy sheen.
Soon will she see Lundavra's woods of fir,
Where lies the house long known and dear to her.
For there abides her father's brother kind
Whose welcome sure she ever hopes to find.
At length the bleak hill-side is well-nigh past
And on a corrie near her eye is cast,
For thicker still the clouds have gathered round,
And on she speeds where shelter may be found.
Ere yet the friendly hollow she can gain,
With rising blast down pours the blinding rain;
But short the distance now, and muffled plaid
And homespun skirt defend the Highland maid.
A few steps more, and down the zig-zag way—
Which never practised footstep did betray—
She reaches soon a deep and quiet nook
Where scarce the breeze some budding rowans shook.
The earth-worn rocky bank o'er-arching bends,
And from the driving storm protection lends:

The wind may blow, and fast the rain may fall,
Here from the tempest is she sheltered all.
She fears but she must long with patience wait,
Nor at Lundavra can arrive till late;
With head on hand, beside a moss-grown stone
She rests, and sighs to feel herself alone.


There falls a quick, light sound upon her ear;
A soft touch on her hand—ah, who is here?
" Oh, Bran, good Bran, thy greetings cheering are,
" For well I know thy master is not far; "
And with a beating heart she, rising, sees—
His belted plaid all waving in the breeze—
Approaching near the young Knight of Lochawe.
" Down, Bran," he cries, " too rough thy kindly paw!
" I scarce can chide him, Mairi: he has read
" My wishes right, altho' my steps he led
" Not altogether willing, to this spot;
" For I was fain our chase should be forgot,

" And thought to check my most sagacious hound
" Whose mute persistence has such quarry found.
" But say, how comes it, dear one, thou art here,
" And thus alone ? "   Then with a rising tear
But steady voice, she simply told her tale,
And much her father's anger did bewail.
" Now am I grateful to the morning breeze
" That warned the herd, and did me then displease;
" For lucky is it that my hard-won chase
" Hath drawn me onward to such distant place.
" I sent the gillies and our spoil by boat,
" As best to reach our bothy so remote.
" Thrice happy then the chance that made me take
" The hill-side way, and for the ferry make.
" Perchance the thought that I might meet a friend
" Persuasion sweet to the intent did lend.
" Now, having met, I'll take my friend to task,
" And answer to repeated question ask—
" How long are these, our childish terms, to last,
" When Love is come to hallow all the past ?

" Oh tell me I am right—do not deny—
" But now I read soft welcome in thine eye,
" That language ever true." " What can I say
" Thou dost not know already in that way?
" A while ago, and I was wae and sad,
" Now thou art here, and Diarmid, I am glad.
" But urge me not—I cannot wed with thee
" Till in such act our kindred fitness see,
" And much I fear these hills will easier move
" Than stubborn wills their prejudice disprove.
" Lochawe's proud Knight I doubt will never meet
" In parlance Callaird's Laird—nor ever greet
" As his, the daughter of a humble foe;
" Thus pride should freeze my heart." "Oh say not so,
" My father loves me well, and when he sees
" No other bride his favourite son can please,
" Consent—tho' tardy—he will surely yield;
" Then we shall grieve that we have aught concealed.
" I'll tell him all, my childish love relate,
" And though his anger may wax stern and great

" At disappointed views—it will be brief,

" And from this weight of secrecy relief

" We then shall know."  "For thy success I pray,

" And all disturbing doubts will chase away.

" Hope is ascendant in thy presence, dear,

" 'Tis but in absence it gives place to fear.

" Yet is there one ne'er on our love will smile,

" Thy haughty chief and kinsman, great Argyll."

" Nay, pale not when dost utter thus his name:

" My clansman's fealty Argyll can claim,

" And honoured service free to him is due;

" Mine eye to serve, my tongue to speak him true,

" My hand to aid, my foot for him pursue,

" And danger's ways mine arm to guide him through,

" My blood to shed, if safer he may live,

" And for his life my very own to give;

" But freedom in my choice to mate is mine,

" And ne'er for frown or smile will I resign

" The precious right to win thy love, and swear

" A higher fealty to thee, nor e'er,

" Forbid it Heaven that I should earn such blame,
" By falsehood to my love his line defame.
" Thine is the service of my heart, I ween,
" For thou, my Mairi, art its chosen queen!"
" Oh Diarmid! sweet it is to hear thy voice
" In words that make my bounding heart rejoice ;
" If my poor self is so much prized by thee,
" Believe that doubly. dear art thou to me ;
" My life's devotion is the sole return
" That I can make—this mayest thou later learn—
" Thy generous love would sure be ill repaid
" Were I the cause of home disunion made ;
" Let but thy parents bless, and I am thine ;
" Thy hope shall be my hope, thy people mine."
" Then shall love's impress seal our compact, dear,
" Nay, would'st thou go ?" " E'en so, yon sky is clear
" And slower move those clouds, but fades the light,
" I needs must haste or be o'erta'en by night."
" We part not till I see thee safe upon
" Thine uncle's homelands near, for I have won

" My suit, and will not leave my promised wife
" To wander lone, but guard her as my life.
" Now wilt thou wear and keep this little spray
" Of myrtle wild, I gathered by the way?
" It is our badge, and by our clan 'tis said,
" ' Put foot thereon, and it will ne'er deceive,'
" Which meaneth—where it grows in safety tread.
" I vouch not for the bog, but this believe,
" That Diarmid will be true."   " I doubt it not,
" Else should unworthy be of such fair lot;
" As soon could I uncertain feel by night
" That with the hour will come returning light,
" As think thou could'st be false!"   "Oh golden day!
" Good augury it was the myrtle spray
" To find; and see, since wearing in my breast,
" Its tender leaves have gratefully confessed
" The vital power of warmth, and sweeter smell;
" Thus to our cherished hopes they joy foretell.
" Despite the chills of worldliness and pride,
" These yet shall strengthen, warmed and sanctified

" By love's all watchful and sustaining care."
" Oh may such forecast sweet fulfilment bear !
" I place thy myrtle in my kerchief deep,
" And when it fades, the withered leaves will keep.
" But not like them shall fade our love's clear light;
" Its fitter emblem rather is yon star
" Through evening gloom just coming into sight :
" In fixed radiance of a world afar
" It shineth ever, tho' unseen by day—
" So shall our love maintain its steadfast way ;
" In darker hours a bright and heaven-sent ray,
" In joy unproved, still beaming none the less—
" Outshone by blaze of noontide happiness."
" Sweet serious one! thy pure fair thoughts take birth
" From holier things, while mine are of the earth.
" But the same Power ordained yon worlds to know
" Their circling orbits—bade the myrtle grow.
" In troublous times, when difficulties bar
" Mine eager steps from thee, be thou the star
" To cheer me on; and when with sunshine blest,

" The fragrant flower to cherish in my breast.

" But hark ! what mean those pipes resounding nigh?"

" They mark where—yonder see—are standing high

" Lundavra's walls, which 'mid those trees appear;

" They tell the labour of the day is done,

" And bid to gather to the evening cheer

" By honest toil and simple service won.

" But little thinks mine uncle that one more

" Will sit his hospitable board before,

" And that through sentence hard and stern, this night

" Will bring to him a niece in homeless plight,

" Dejected and alone."   " Say but the word,

" I thee accompany, from this deterred

" By nought save thine own self."   " 'Twere best not so,

" And seemlier of our meeting none should know.

" Quick tongues might bear it to thy father's ear,

" And it would justly anger him to hear

" From rumour vague, what thine own lips should tell;

" So now farewell."   " My heart's best wealth, farewell.

" Yet stay—how, when are we again to meet?"

" I know not, but shall live in dreaming sweet
" Of that blest hour."   " May Heaven propitious prove
" And grant it soon.   Good Angels guard my love."


The lovers leaving to their parted ways—
O'er which would each oft cast a backward gaze—
Return we now unto the aged crone
Whose feeble steps, as yet observed by none,
Have to the ferry brought her tardily,
Thus far attained in patience wearily.
" I would Glencoe side reach, and, Sir, would fain
" A passage straightway in thy boat obtain."
" Now who art thou, our maiden's plaid who wears?
" Such sight unwonted, air of mystery bears ;
" Some evil hath befallen its owner, sure,
" Or how that tartan could'st thou else procure ?
" Thou wilt not speak ! then to the laird must go ;
" 'Tis fit of this strange hazard he should know."

And in the homestead soon the laird is found,
His orders issuing to the menials round.
" Whom bring'st thou here?" "A stranger all unsought
" Is thus into thine honoured presence brought;
" She weareth, as thou seest, thy daughter's plaid,
" And when thereon I observation made,
" Demanding how it came that one of lot
" So humble had such goodly raiment got,
" No word could I, nor any answer gain;
" She doth a silence obstinate maintain."
" Nay, mistress, why is this?"    " To thee I speak;
" I met a damsel on the hillside bleak,
" Who pity took upon mine aged frame,
" And did what angel would, nor Heaven will blame;
" She gave me of her plaid one half to wear,
" And see. the rough-cut end doth witness bear
" To these my words."    " In sooth 'tis even so,
" For by the tartan's length thou speakest truth.
" Poor Mairi in her folly aye will go
" And lose herself—thus may her simple youth

" By ill be overcome ; now do I see
" 'Tis useless quite, she ne'er will wiser be,
" But have her way ; so when the morn is come,
" Go seek her out, and bring my daughter home."


Then with the early dawn, Lundavra's door,
With hasty tread a gillie came before,
And speech with Mairi sought.   She heard him there
But heeded not the message that he bare.
Unwilling felt she now the home to seek
Whence spurned with words, had crushed a spirit meek.
He much entreated, till her uncle came
The question to discuss, and urged the same.
Still was she loth, and long they her besought,
Ere mingled prayers and chidings on her wrought
Consent to yield ; then homeward slow she turned,
In sorrow for life's hardening lesson—learned.


They met her kindly, and they spoke her fair,
But ah, a wounded spirit who can bear !

Thenceforward, saddened by the harshness dealt,
As alien in her family she dwelt ;
Consorting scarce with those who might upbraid,
In turret room remote she oftenest staid.
Thus came it she was sharer never in
The gleesome ways that youthful spirits win
To merriment ; from these excluded all,
In lone monotony she lived apart,
And in fond hope of good that might befal,
And musings sweet, beguiled an aching heart.


Up Linnhe sailed a ship from Eastern parts,
Well stored with merchandise of foreign marts.
In shelter of the Point it anchorage found:
Ere long from far and near folk gathered round,
The lading to inspect, and all would fain
Some products rare with little coin obtain.
Much goodly work was there, and longing eyes
Were cast on linens fine and precious dyes ;

These last most coveted as means to shade
The native wools their homewove tartan made.
Then they of Callaird on the sight were bent,
And all, save Mairi, soon on shipboard went.
Strange things were shown, inspected and approved,
And some they chose forthwith to be removed.
A chest apart the laird discovered then—
" What is therein ?  Why keep it from our ken ?"
" Good sir, if I withhold it from thy view
" 'Tis but that the contents are not quite new,
" Altho' of silks and rich apparel rare,
" And gauds befitting royalty to wear ;
" I raise the lid—so—now wilt partly see
" The braveries within."  " And what may be
" The price demanded for this half-worn gear ?
" If moderate, then a purchaser is here."
The bargain's struck right soon—as aye hath been
When they who sell, and those would buy, are keen
Possessions to exchange.  The money paid,
And all well pleased with acquisitions made,

The party speedily the house regain,
And straight begin themselves to entertain
With closer view and more entire display
Of finery obtained—and in this way
Was soon apportioned to each one a share,
Which all in pride began forthwith to wear.
But Mairi in their pleasure had no part,
Shut out, it so befel, by thoughtless art;
Nor was her presence sought, since all declared
For richer garments that she never cared.
'Twas useless quite to give such like to her
Who never aught could keep, and would incur
Fresh chiding certes with occasion given.
" She cannot come—I have the bolt hard driven
" Of door into her room—there must she wait."
Thus, half in jest, half childish petulance
The little brother spoke. His early fate
Just wrath disarms—a terrible mischance
Soon laid him low, and on that household fell.
The rich habiliments which keen to sell

Had been the owner, danger all unknown
To dwellers in these mountain districts lone,
Evil unwonted and undreamt of, wrought;
The young and gay had worn them, with no thought
Of misery that might be handed down
To other wearers—the brocaded gown,
Embroidered cloth, those braveries all, bore
Infecting taint the merchant did ignore.
And now, new-worn, the poison that still lurked
Among their folds, a quick destruction worked.
Thus then it fell, ere many hours were past,
That signs of grievous sickness showed, which cast
Mysterious blight on the three youngest born.
In glee they donned again, th' ensuing morn,
The chosen finery which the eve before
Had been assigned to them; they strewed the floor
With silks that to their eyes seemed gayest, best,
From out the open and still well-filled chest;
The brothers in this pastime also shared,
And peering oft, the serving-folk declared

Loud admiration of the novelties
Displayed to view. Soon were their sympathies
In other and in sadder ways required.
The joyous spirits that were flagging, tired,
And wailing took the place of laughter hushed;
For cheeks with fever, 'stead of mirth, were flushed,
And restless limbs lay tossing on the bed.
All efforts made to soothe the aching head,
The sudden pangs, were vain—the rising sun
Looked in on pallid forms, on havoc done :
It shone on growing terrors and on ill
That waxed to agonies increasing still.
The Leech quick sought for, came—in horror saw
That skill was powerless, and fled in awe.
Soon spread his dire report throughout the glen,
And great was fear and consternation then.
What visitation were they doomed to see ?
" Black Death," the foul Black Death, it sure must be.
Of such appalling foe what need to tell
The rapid stride, or how contagion fell

Through that affrighted stricken household ran,
And snapped the threads of Life's uncertain span,
Till father, children, servitors were seized,
Ere was the fury of that plague appeased.
Another night, another rising sun,
And Azrael's solemn mission there was done.


Oh Death ! thou sure avenger of the past,
O'er which thy mantle dark is sternly cast.
Oh thou that takest spirits loved away,
And forms so dear dost turn to inert clay ;
Thou terror vague of all the earth have trod !
Pale visitant ! dread messenger of God !
Fain would we flee—fain from thy touch would shrink,
That leadeth far o'er this known planet's brink.
The shadow of thy presence falls upon
Our dearest, and its mien they sadly don,
As hour by hour thy coming draws more near,
And those who watch await in awe and fear.

What doth this darkening nearness hide from sight?
No light, no shadow—then if shadow, light—
Thy mighty gloom need not affright the mind,
For everlasting glory shines behind.
Faith hears thy call, and gives the trembling hand.
The eye is closed on all life could command,
The soul is wafted on a parting sigh,
The mortal lost in Immortality.


But how, the while, had time with Mairi sped,
So near, yet sundered from such danger dread?
The prank in frolic played, her safeguard proved.
Long in her chamber lone she heard unmoved
The usual sounds of life and stir below,
Which loudly told the party had returned
From ploy it cost her little to forego.
She sighed not for mere pleasure, but she yearned
For sympathy, and this she could not find
Within her home. Though not devoid of love,

Her kindred uncongenial were in mind,
By motives swayed, her spirit soared above.
Thus locked within herself, for ever dumb
On one dear name—so used had she become
To thoughts and occupations all her own,
That solitude to her had pleasing grown.
Yet of such isolation she would tire
At times, and sweet companionship desire.
Therefore much more from weariness of heart
Than of the body, minding scarce to touch
The evening fare prepared with simple art
And at her hand, she early sought her couch.


Not then until the morn was far advanced
Did she in part discover what had chanced.
Her wonderment at finding egress barred
First filled her with alarm, then rudely jarred
Against her sense of justice. Why was this?
What did it mean? Was it with grave intent

Or but in mischief done? On freedom bent
She called, but called in vain. Ah, when they miss
Her presence, some one surely will come near
To seek her out, and mystery make clear.
So gently turning from the door again,
In hope perchance the notice to obtain
Of passer-by, she placed herself beside
The open casement, whence might be descried
The narrow track that up the mountain led.
It was but seldom strangers' foot would tread
That rugged path, and labourers of the soil
As rarely took that road to seek their toil.
Th' ascent just there was rougher and more steep;
Pursuing huntsman must with caution creep,
Though lightly might the roe o'er hindrance leap.
About the foot would lime and chesnut lend
Much fragrant shade, and upward in the bend
Did fir with ash and birch its foliage blend.
Tho' bounded, 'twas a scene in sunshine fair
To look upon, and now when sitting there,

She mentally retraced the steps she took
The day when, haunted by that angry look,
She sadly trod the mountain path alone,
And such extremes of pain and joy had known.
How changed to her had life and all things been
Since that last day when she had Diarmid seen.
As they were wont, her musings fondly dwelt
Upon his words, his looks—for him she felt
Affection daily more engrossing still,
Which adverse circumstances could not chill.
Ah! lowering seemed the future, dark with fear,
With scarce a ray of light the gloom to cheer.
But he had bid her hope, and in him trust—
She would do both, believe in him she must ;
And in that faith she wandered far away
By fantasy beguiled, nor did she stay
Her fingers from the wheel. So passed the day
Till evening came upon her unaware,
Lost in sweet reveries, forgetting care.
A soft delicious melancholy stole

Upon her senses and enwrapped her soul :
It seemed as though a crisis in her fate
Were near—and one than others thought of less.
What might not mean those feelings that of late
Had so oppressed her ;  languor, weariness,
Those piercing thrills, those tremors of the heart ?
Might not these warnings be that she must part
From earthly hopes, and e'en the firmest ties
Must loosen, and from human weakness rise ?
And were it so—were she indeed to die,
Would he forget,  or would he sometimes sigh
In soft remembrance of her love for him ?
At memory's picture would his eye grow dim—
She strove to think of him with one beside,
As walking with that other, nobler bride,
His father so desired to see him wed :
One who seemed fitter far with him to tread
Life's devious course—who would as equal meet
His people, nor their favour need entreat.
Her fancy painted him in future years

The centre of affection's hopes and fears,
And with such brightness and such good endowed
As scarce permitted fleeting grief to cloud
The sunshine of his days.   Yet might thro' all
At times a sigh be breathed, a tear let fall
For Mairi dead—well did her heart aver
That Heaven itself could not be Heaven for her
If consciousness of him ne'er entered there;
Or entering, showed that she forgotten were.
But why torment the mind with futile strife,
Is not our love immortal as our life !
To doubt such soothing hope were agony.
A voice and ear attuned to harmony
In truest measure did to her belong,
And now her thoughts broke forth in plaintive song.

### SONG.

When voices glad make gay the hall
  And fairy forms are flitting past
With smiling lip and merry call,
  And kindly looks around are cast;

When climbing on thy knee,
Thy baby heir looks fondly up
    And clasps thy neck with tiny power,
And mutual love fills full thy cup
    Of happiness—in that sweet hour,
        A moment think of me.

When storm is past, and clear the sky
    Serenely shows as daylight fades,
And zephyr fans with faintest sigh
    Caressingly; when lengthening shades
        Come creeping o'er the lea,
And mavis on its leafy perch
    Sits carolling sweet notes aloft,
From chesnut bough or slender birch,
    The listening ear beguiling oft—
        Then sometimes think of me.

When shining high, the Queen of Night
    Pale splendour casts o'er glade and hill,
And marks a path of silver light
    O'er ocean waves all hushed and still;
        When falls her power on thee,
And calmness steals into thine heart,
    And griefs and cares as nothing seem—
So great is felt His wondrous part,
    A world who formed and did redeem—
        Then think, oh, think of me.

Sleep gives new vigour—with returning light
She rose more cheerful; youthful hopes were stronger
And gone the shadows of the previous night.
Prisoning so strange can scarcely last much longer,
Since likely it was caused, so she supposed,
By childish folly; still is firmly closed
All power of exit; she will wait unmoved,
And thus should patience from within wear out
The irritating teasing from without:
So best unruly spirits be reproved.
She had no lack of food, for there was stored
In a well-shelved recess, a simple hoard
Of meal, of honey, and of rustic fare
Which she was used with poverty to share.
She sat her down to her accustomed wheel,
And busy at her work, soon ceased to feel
Uneasy, nay, ere long, forgot annoyance.
Lulled by the whirring sound her labour caused,
The hours went calmly by until she paused,
Roused by some signs below of dire disturbance.

She listens—wonted noises sure had changed,
And seemed domestic order disarranged;
An anxious call, a hurried step, a moan,
Confusion more—and now a louder groan!
" What turmoil strange is this? and ah, that shriek!
" Another, and yet more!　Oh, some one speak!
" Undo this door that bars me in so strong,
" I would go help—there must be grievous wrong—
" Will no one hear ?"　Again the door she tries,
And calls, but words are lost in shriller cries.
In hearing thus of mortal agony
The wail, in wild suspense the night crept by,
And with the dawn fresh efforts made she still
Imprisonment to break—with frantic will,
Though strength all-impotent.　Pausing she leans
And looks around.　That iron bar a means
Suggests by which escape may be attained—
If rightly she but use the force thus gained.
She takes it and inserts the narrow end
In crevice of the door she hopes to rend;

Oh why, why not have thought of this before?
The panel yields—another wrench—one more,
And lo, the staple falls, the way is free,
The weary prisoner is at liberty.
Wherefore this silence in the house below?
Stillness her ear had ne'er been used to know.
The narrow winding stair in nameless dread
She hurries down, to where it stopped and led
To the main portion of the dwelling quaint;
She hears no sound, no murmur of complaint.
The angle past, oh, horror to behold,
Before her lay her father, stiff and cold!
Death in the livid face, the half-closed eyes,
The rigid form that all distorted lies;
Death in most hideous aspect loathsome seen.
With startled gaze and terror-stricken mien,
As petrified, she stands a moment there,
Unable to descend the further stair:
That prostrate body never can she pass.
A rush of thoughts come crowding on her brain:

Where now the iron will she had been fain
In all humility to fear—alas !
Alas ! when living he had thrust her forth ;
Now dead, he held her in—with silent power
Which awed her more than animated wrath.
Tho' dark was *that* still darker is *this* hour.
Let come what may, she must endure her doom ;
She turned and fled up to her turret room,
With trembling hand shut close the riven door,
Then tottering, fell in swoon upon the floor.


When on that morn no sign of life, no stir
Was seen within the house or round about,
Some few approached, whom fear could not deter,
And questioning terror spread the land throughout.
" All dead within—how then was heard that cry ?
" But faint the sound.  We dare not go to see,
" For blackening corpses near the threshold lie.
" What can be done to stay this misery ?"

All horror-stricken, quick, with hurried feet
The tenants of the land in council meet.
" For burial then, if none will lend a hand—
" And such a service we can scarce demand
" Of any man—some other method we
" Must straight devise, and this our firm decree- -
" The house must be burnt down, and cleansing fire
" Shall all consume on one funereal pyre ;
" And to ensure contagion shall not spread
" Beyond that doomed abode of many dead,
" All boats which now upon Glencoe side lie
" Shall on Lochaber shore be hauled up high ;
" So no one can to Callaird pass meantime :
" Such act forbidden shall be deemed a crime.
" Great watch-fires must be lit around by night
" On ' Piper's,' ' Carnaich ' Point, on Callaird's height,
" On Kenneth's Isle, Port Eachin, head of lake,
" At ' Strait of hounds '—thus all approaches make
" Impassable.  And further we ordain—
" Whoso shall to the house set fire, by lot

" Shall chosen be ; nor leave that loathsome spot
" Within a given time, on certain pain
" Of instant death.  By measures these preventing
" Worse harm, and with all prudence circumventing;
" We hope to master and stamp out, the ill.
" Now cast the lots, and see who must fulfil
" This act of duty to his fellow-men."
'Tis done.  It falls on Iain of the Glen,
On Iain Mór, in Callaird bravest, best,
The " piper's man's wee laddie " called in jest.
" I will in all fidelity obey
" Your wise behest.  But let me first, I pray,
" Make sure that no one breathes those walls within ;
" So may not on my conscience lie the sin
" Of murder."   " It is well.  None long can live
" In that dread charnel-house : this scarce need give
" Thy troubled thoughts much anguish, for the deed
" Is righteous—in which true belief we plead
" With Heaven for help to crown it with success.
" May that just Heaven protect thee aye and bless.

" Thus armed, go forth, and when no answering call,
" No wailing sound upon thine ear shall fall,
" Then quickly do thy part.   Now all away,
" For each has work admits of no delay." .


The shades of coming night were gathering fast
When Iain neared the house, and quickly passed
The entrance by; with watchful eye and ear
And caution moved he, not unmixed with fear.
As by the northern side he wandered round,
There still no sign of life, no slightest sound ;
But at the further end a casement high
Was open wide—and on the sill did lie,
Prone on the folded arms all white and bare,
A head bowed down as tho' in mute despair.
He calls " Ho, there ! Oh speak, if any live !"
The hills in mocking echoes answer give.
With fixed gaze, in breathless awe he waits,
Half startled at the clamour he creates.

His voice has roused the strong life-seeking will
Which in that frame exhausted lingers still :
Yes, there is movement, and the head is raised.
" Oh Iain, is it thou ?   Great Heaven be praised !
" A friend at last !   Help and deliverance now
" Are surely come.   Oh tell me, tell me how
" Has all this 'wildering horror come about ?
" I faint with fear ; beseech thee, help me out."
" Alack the day, dost thou not see and know
" That death abideth in the house below ?
" Art thou alone ?"   " Alone these four long days;
" And all last night, with anguish and amaze,
" I heard but groans and shrieks, and sounds of pain
" I'd fain have soothed, but strove to reach in vain,
" For by some hazard rare or strange forecast,
" My chamber door was from without made fast ;
" And 'spite endeavours wild the bolt to break,
" Resisted every effort I could make,
" Till morning light a way suggesting, brought
" Release at length.   The liberty I thought  ·

" Thus to have gained, did but augment my woe.

" With headlong haste I rushed me down, when lo!

" Across the stair and barring me the way,

" My father's lifeless body prostrate lay.

" Ah, horrible the sight—aghast I fled,

" And here forsaken bide in trembling dread.

" I dare not go to look upon that face,

" Nor can I pass to get me from the place;

" I call, but no one comes—there is no sound,

" Nought but a silence awful and profound;

" What has befallen, say, oh say." " Alas!

" The hand of God hath ruin brought to pass

" Upon the house of Callaird. Fell disease

" Hath swept it through, in manner as doth freeze

" The blood to think on. Of 'the Black Death' they died,"

" And in thy veins, as is most like, doth hide

" The same destroying taint." " Ah, woe is me!

" In all its hideous peril now I see

" My dread position—still I fain would live,

" And be at large. Though none dare house-room give,

" I'd shelter in the woods and have no fear.

" In mercy sure some angel sent thee here."

" Poor prisoner, I am here intent to do

" A fearful duty such as man ne'er knew.

" 'Twas thought no life within these walls remained,

" Or long could linger—therefore all contained

" Therein, with them, the rulers have ordained

" Be burnt with fire—laid level with the ground.

" Command is laid on me, by lot thus bound

" To do the deed, whene'er no answering sound

" Shall reach mine ear; nor leave the place till done."

" And what the penalty if left undone ?"

" The penalty of death."    " And must I die?

" Must all my hopes end in a shrieking sigh ?

" This breathing body soon in ashes lie?

" Oh horror past belief!   Oh, Iain Mòr,

" Befriend me still.   Thy pity I implore.

" Could Diarmid of Lochawe but knowledge have

" Of this my dire distress, perchance to save

" He'd find the way.   I do entreat thee, seek

" Him out, and howsoe'er this ends, oh speak

" With him, and tell of all this misery.

" A farewell blessing take to him from me.

" I know his truth and courage would not fail

" If o'er my piteous lot they could prevail.

" Ah me, were he but here !"   " The place around

" A watch is stationed : none dare pass that bound.

" But these wide-set precautions may prove vain

" Against a bold resolve its end to gain ;

" For much a loyal heart can dare and do,

" If armed with motive strong to bear it through.

" Lochawe is far—if there my foot but reach

" I scarce can fail with Diarmid to get speech.

" Then bravely rest thee in this patient trust,

" For now through Night's enwrapping veil I must

" With prudence haste.   If Heaven my purpose bless

" The morrow's night may bring thee happiness.

" Then pray for me : thy mind in calmness keep,

" In hope and courage, so let terrors sleep."

That very hour the watch his post forsook,
And, unobserved, the speediest way he took
To Inverawe, but whether o'er the hill,
By boat or by the glen, is unknown still.
Howbeit that through night he went is true,
So Highland thews and Highland will could do.


Lochawe's young Knight has dreamed a horrid dream,
Wherein did Mairi sad and tearful seem ;
By dangers wild and terrible beset.
Long weeks had slowly passed since last they met,
And now strange fears for her disturb repose.
With restless and uneasy mind he rose,
Then with intention quick his horse he sought,
And straightway sallied forth in anxious thought.
The hour was early—few were yet astir,
As up the river's course he went his way
By mingled groups of chesnut, beech, and fir,
Which, either side adorning, scattered lay,

Their foliage heavy with the glistening dew.
Short time Lochawe's fair surface brought to view,
Half hid in morning mist; of sombre hue
The scene appeared, by reason of the deep
Far-reaching shadow thrown around by steep
And rugged hills—a curtain flung o'er sleep
Of waters which the growing power of light
Will gently lift, and beauty bring to sight,
And stir of life. On rocky islet near,
Two mighty birds stood forth in outline clear;
Huge eagles, fiercest of the feathered race,
Presiding seemed like monarchs of the place.
As though the treading of his horse's feet
Disturbed the wonted quiet of their seat,
They rose, and with a steady, measured flight,
Slow winged their way towards Cruachan's stony height.
Anon the tired pedestrian, Iain Mór,
With look of haste the rider comes before,
And each, unknowing of the other, made
Such courteous salutation as was paid

Whilome by every Celt.  " All hail to thee
" Good stranger : sight unwonted 'tis to see
" One of such hurried step and air distraught.
" Say, whither goest thou ?"  " Through Night I've sought,
" Spite hindrance frequent, Inverawe to gain,
" With young Lochawe short parlance to obtain ;
" From far Lochaber's side in pressing need
" I come, help seeking."  " Thither with all speed
" My way I take.  Prithee thy purpose tell."
" Fair sir, I fain would in thy favour dwell,
" But words like mine must be for Diarmid's ear
" And his alone."  " Nay, speak man, without fear,
" For I am he."  " Events of crushing grief
" Have come to pass—a message sad and brief
" I bear to thee from one who hapless lies
" In utmost peril.  Callaird's daughter sighs
" Her lonely life away."  " Oh, cruel fate !
" Whate'er they be, thy tidings quick relate."
Then did that trusty emissary tell
His tale of woe, and how it all befel ;

How Mairi was in loathsome durance fast
And long imprisoned, durance that must last
Till freed therefrom by death of fearful kind,
Unless some fertile brain could means devise
Which daring hand should promptly realise,
And win her freedom : How a watch was set
Approaches to secure, and make outlet
Scarce possible ; how stern the penalty
Awaiting any who should wilfully
The edict break. " Now by the Heaven above,
" I'll venture all to free my 'prisoned love,
" Or perish in the attempt ! Say, new-found friend,
" Unto my project wilt thou furtherance lend
" To save this luckless girl ?" " With heart and hand
" I'll do that same—my every nerve command."
" Then part we here—first rest thee for a space
" While we concert a plan requiring skill
" And hardihood. When I my steps retrace
" For instant work, do thou across the hill
" Betake thee quick ; none art thou like to meet

" Upon its rugged track.  At nightfall greet
" The poor unhappy captive's waiting ear
" With words of hope the sinking heart to cheer :
" Tell her, God willing, Diarmid will be near,
" And with him means of rescue.  Bid her not
" Despond; she shall from such appalling lot
" Be saved in way that ne'er shall be forgot."


Soon fiery Diarmid on his homeward way
Is urging fast his sure and willing grey.
Of such unusual trampling at the sound
Peep prying heads from humble dwellings round :
The slow unskilful tiller of the soil,
The gillie hastening to his morning toil,
Turn them in silent wonderment, at sight
Of the demeanour strange of their young Knight.
" Ho, Hamish, is it thou?  Come hither, lad,
" To meet thee thus I am in truth right glad.
" I know thou well canst pull an oar.  I need

" Some gallant help to do a daring deed.

" Wilt come with me ?"    " Full willingly I go."

" Then find me Duncan, Neil, Macdougal, Lowe,

" And other three, for I have work for all.

" Haste, bid them meet me at the Boathouse Fall,

" Their labour leave at once, nor doubting halt ;

" I'll be their surety, should they prove in fault."

Onward the grey, and off the gillie sped.

When gained the precincts of the lordly tower

The rider left his horse within a shed

And by a postern passing, sought the bower

Where was his sister wont her flowers to tend,

Or with her feathered pets such time to spend ;

And as he neared, he heard her voice in song.

She stops, " What is it, Diarmid, what is wrong ?"

" Oh, Clare, I am in sore distress of mind,

" And hither come thy gentle help to find.

" Give me, I pray thee, a full wearing suit

" Of thine apparel."    " 'Tis a strange request."

" And wouldst thou too my Venice lace and lute,

" Or will my simplest home-gear serve thee best?
" This seemeth like some foolish prank of thine,
" In borrowed plumes to make some lassie shine.
" Think, Diarmid, what thou dost : I know 'tis said
" A certain Cameron damsel thou wouldst wed."
" To bandy words I have no will, no power ;
" I tell thee, Life and Death hang on the hour.
" Help if thou wilt what thou dost call my freak,
" Or what I need perforce I'll elsewhere seek."
" I was but jesting, frown not, brother dear ;
" All thou dost need I'll bring, so wait thou here,"
And with a smile she vanished as she spoke.
The minutes passed in silence all unbroke
Save for the hurried steps with which he paced
The pretty sunny room that southward faced.
He threw a glance impatiently around,
If haply aught of interest might be found.
Wandering it fell upon a heavy tome
Wherein, it would appear, had been whilome
His sister reading—not unknown the book,

And drawing near, a reverential look
He cast upon the wide and open page,
In humble trust thus sorrows to assuage,
Did any ever gaze thereon in vain?
" Thou shalt not be afraid" of killing pain,
Nor of the pestilence that walks by night.—
This the assurance strong that met his sight.
It calmed him, and when Clare returned right soon,
And with her brought the strangely-needed boon,
He thanked her with a gentle kindly word,
Which yet with anxious fear her heart bestirred.
" Oh, Diarmid, what art thou about to do?
" Sadly this day my thoughts will thee pursue."
" Then let them follow me with loving prayer
" That full success may crown the deed I dare
" Forthwith to do. In peril of her life,
" In woe, lies one I fain would make my wife."
" Ah, do not rashly what thou mayst too late
" Repent. Thy father's son should never mate
" With one of humble birth." " I tell thee, Clare,

" She's nature's gentlewoman, good as fair;

" And if I bring her safe from every harm,

" Confiding in her worth and simple charm,

" Could'st thou not rise all prejudice above,

" And greet this stranger with a sister's love ? "

" Oh, loth were I to think that to such act

" Mere beauty's magnet could thy love attract.

" Or e'er that thou could'st link with lower mind,

" And in its fellowship contentment find.

" Therefore I take on trust right willingly

" This maid as worthy of thyself; if be

" In very truth thy happiness at stake,

" Then, Diarmid, I will love her for thy sake."

" There spoke my own sweet sister.  Ask me not

" What means I try to save her from hard lot;

" I cannot wait to tell, but must away,

" For much have I to do ere close of day."


Then by the hazel bank and brackens tall
He hasted, till he reached the Boathouse Fall,

Where, to his joy, he found assembled all;
Eight stalwart gillies, by his summons brought,
His lead to follow with no questioning thought.
" Brave lads, well know I ye'll my bidding do :
" My scheme I'll tell while we our course pursue.
" Launch now the birlinn light, and quick prepare
" Ye for some roughish work; and for our fare,
" Let him of fleetest foot go, hither bring
" Provision that will last a two days' trip.
" See there—these wrappers by the tiller fling,
" And trim the boat, the bow needs deeper dip."
Brief space is needed when men work with will,
And each his different part performs with skill.
" All ready," and the widening stream along,
The birlinn flies, impelled by rowers strong,
Whose oars soon Etive cleave. " How serves the tide ? "
" It suiteth well, once Rudha Fionn outside,
" A northward run will quick and easy be."
" Then all hands pull until the narrows through,
" And passed the points, we gain the fav'ring sea;

" There we may slacken speed—one-half my crew
" Awhile should from their willing labour rest,
" Not to exhaust their strength—thus may we best
" Our scene of enterprise by nightfall reach."


The oars are plied with telling might, for each
Is wielded by a practised arm of force.
The Connal Falls are passed, and on its course
The boat speeds sure, and breasts the briny deep.
Upon the left hand shore Dunstaffnage Keep
On rocky point stands boldly forth and clear
Against the sky. " Pull steady, lads, for here
" A jabble we shall have of crossing sea,
" Which we must face, till under Lismore Lea
" We row with ease, helped onward by the tide."
In silence buffet they the billows' play
Until, the headland rounded, soon they glide
In smoother waters, and make rapid way:
" Now, easy all, and take the work in turn,

" While from your leader ye his project learn."
They hear with interest, and with zeal accede
To hazard life, so be the prisoner freed.

Poor captive—how with her doth creep the hour!
Oh for magnetic or volition's power
To whisper hope, and tell help cometh fast!
The boat moves on—now Appin rocks are past,
And Shuna's Isle aye clearer shows ahead,
Where freely is the eye on beauty fed.
The midday sun pours in unclouded might
On the reflecting waters—dazzling sight,
Which finds relief along the changing shore,
Where nature lavishes so rich a store
Of forms and hues; the loitering wanderer there
Hears in the balmy and untroubled air
The sound of straining oars, which measure keep,
Borne o'er the rippling wavelets' noontide sleep.
He casts a look of calm inquiry o'er
The shining surface, and he marks where soar

Those sea-mews startled from their rocky perch
By passing of yon distant boat—in search
Most like of finny prey, though an advance
So steady, graver purpose had, perchance.
Onward it speeds —the birds returning, flock
Around, resettling on their favourite rock;
And those within the boat small heed bestow
On objects which, if erstwhile seen, would glow
Of pleasure bring into their sportsman's eye.
The slumbering seals all disregarded lie
In far-off whiteness on the dark low line
That breaks the gleaming plain—some instinct fine
Wakes apprehension's sense at faintest sound,
And sliding from the rock in sudden fear,
A sure retreat is instantaneous found
Within the depths of watery covert near.
At varying intervals black heads uprise
And gaze with large and melancholy eyes
On the receding cause of fancied harm
Which their siesta broke with vague alarm.

Unswervingly the birlinn thus pursues
Her even course—the rowers' vigorous thews
At length are conscious of opposing power
More taxing strength, which marks the turning hour
Of Linnhe's tide.  It ebbs.  A weary spell
Of heavy work must come, they know full well.
Courage, stout hearts, and prove your metal true;
The way is long, but nerve will bear ye through.


The sun was low ere rose Ardsheal to view,
The spirits cheering of the patient crew.
Yet doth it seem that point they ne'er could round,
For here the current is e'en stronger found.
Stanchly these brave ones toil the waves upon,
And daylight wanes, while still the boat creeps on.
One half-hour more, and soon the tide will turn—
The headland passing, thence they can discern
The light on Piper's point.  "In sight at last!
" If but that guarded entrance can be passed.

" Now land we at the first convenient spot
" Where 'tis most like some hayropes may be got
" With which to bind our oars and muffle sound."
Macdougal speaks " By Leitir's Farm, the ground
"I know right well; could we up yonder creek
" But run, then Neil and I would fodder seek."
They row to shore—those on the foray sent
Return full soon, 'neath bulky burdens bent,
Which in the boat they stow, and quick arrange
The order of their work ; as, how to change
The rowers, when the bindings worn out grew,
Which those not pulling, should with care renew.
And thus prepared—in cover of the night
They stealthily approach the point where bright
The beacon shines, and as they nearer gain,
They voices hear of noisy loiterers, fain
To stay with those who watch beside the fire ;
And all discourse with tongues that never tire.
If sounds there are, these idlers hear them not,
And their eyes, dazzled by the blazing spot

Of brightness near—amid the darkness round,
Perceive not the mysterious darker line
Aye stealing on, until its way has wound
Beneath the rock whereon they lounge supine.
To breathe the bold intruders scarcely dare,
But keeping close, beyond the spreading glare,
They face the Carnuis point, where also glows
A warning light which further danger shows.
In ghostly silence they advance—the brave
Win Fortune's smile, denied to faltering slave.
Yet nearer drift they—little need to row,
For favoured by the fast incoming flow
Of waters, skill is most required to guide
The birlinn so she clear the rocky side.
She touches, and tho' slight the sound, 'tis heard
By some above, for here too is a crowd
Of flitting forms, although in talk less loud.
"What noise was that below? Sure something stirred,
"Oh hearken well!" "Nay, friend, I nothing hear,
"Maybe 'twas but some otter loosed a stone

" Which rolling fell. The flow has stronger grown
" And ripples more. In night so calm and clear,
" Oft trifling sounds into importance swell,
" And fancy heareth more than they would tell.
" Methinks the fire doth somewhat feebly glow
" And fuel needs—then pine-logs bring, and throw
" More furze thereon." The unseen listeners wait
Breathless, and marvel what may be their fate.
All motionless, with throbbing pulse, and tongue
So parched that speech therefrom could ill be wrung,
They watch the moments as they pass, so brief,
Yet long to them. With sense of quick relief,
They hear the steps retreating from the bank,
And with an earnest, voiceless prayer, they thank
The Power protecting—Diarmid prompt has laid
His hand on the projecting rock, that made
Risk imminent—he stays their further move
Till is withdrawn attention from above;
Then with a push—through darkness on they glide
Safe past ! 'Tis easier now, the loch more wide,

Still is a fire on Kenneth's Isle descried,
So cautiously the muffled oars are plied,
While for the Ferry's landing place they make.
How faint soe'er the sounds that softly break
The perfect stillness of the midnight air,
They reach the ear of lonely watcher there :
And when on shore they would attempt to land,
He meets them with repelling stern demand
" Who are ye, Sirs ?   None here may step on shore !
" It is debarred, for cause we all deplore."
" Good man, thy prohibition need'st not speak,
" For I am Diarmid of Lochawe, and seek
" To save a life from out yon dwelling foul.
" Were all the fiends of pestilence to howl
" With living tongues defiance to my will,
" Yet would I on—and dauntless, dare them still."
" Sir knight, I honour much thy gallant heart
" And ne'er to such will play betrayer's part;
" But I am set a duty here to do ;
    And should I fail, sad mischief may ensue.

" I but entreat that thou wilt land alone,

" And suffer these may in the boat remain

" While thou thy venture bold dost strive to gain :

" Thus much I ask for my compliance shown."

" Agreed, so friends, push off, and wait my call ;

" I will return accompanied, or fall

" In Love's sweet service."   And alone he speeds

By the shore path that to the dwelling leads,

By rocky turnings, and then upwards wending,

The slope where blooms the yellow whin ascending ;

When one advances whom he joys to know,

For Iain's voice he hears in challenge low.

" Who is it comes ? "   " 'Tis I, our entrance won ;

" Seemed it as tho' the day would ne'er be done,

" Such hours we've had of weariness and toil,

" To reach this place from which all men recoil.

" But Mairi ? "   " Lives, and prays for sight of thee !

" Low bends my heart, altho' not now my knee

" In deepest gratitude.   Quick, let us haste,

" Nor longer these too precious moments waste."

We vary in our estimate of time
As widely as we range in roving thought
Between the frivolous and the sublime;
As strangely as our thread of life is wrought
Into a web of hues contrasting strong,
Yet which the richest tints are found among,
When deeper tracings with them interlace.
The moments, as the years, in even pace
Move on—so fixed, they bring us good or hurt,
In course we cannot hasten or avert.
To ardent youth, though day by day flies fast,
A round of seasons seems a long forecast;
And middle life a period so removed
We cannot think thereon until 'tis proved.
That epoch passed, then shows in saddening truth
Each decade less than seemed a year in youth.
Unto the gay and happy, rosy hours
Flit by unmarked, in safe and sunny bowers;
But to the weak, the troubled and the sad,
Not so—with them the minutes scarce are glad;

And hours creep by, and days, yet is their measure
Stern and unchanged, alike in pain and pleasure.
The weary heart on hope deferred long fed;
The suffering sick, the dying on their bed;
The wounded hero on the battle-field
In dread of foeman's thrust, bereft of shield;
Th' enduring brave, awaiting surgeon's knife;
The criminal condemned within his cell,
Knowing the morn must bring the fatal knell;—
These in such hours must live an age of life,
And, realised the vanity of Earth,
Will look on Death but as a second birth.


Or soon or late there comes a ruling hour
To all, when grave reflection claims her power.
Such came there now unto the captive maid,
Who still to loneliness and woe consigned,
Long for endurance and for rescue prayed.
As gentle Hope beguiled the tortured mind,

Short slumber visited her aching brain,
And in oblivion's calm it lulled the pain.
Thus with repose, her strength renewing, blest,
She lay till dawn broke in upon her rest.
"Ah, has he found him?" was her waking thought,
Which with it rushing all her miseries brought.
But what her fate should Diarmid absent be—
Such dread mischance she will not dare foresee.
She tries to calculate the time would need
Her messenger, that toilsome length to gain
Which, obstacles apart, the utmost speed
Of active manhood must severely strain.
Imagination set before her all
The course of incidents that might befal;
The seeking, meeting, telling of her woe,
—Some way to help would Diarmid surely know;
It conjured up his sorrow for her sake
And pictured every step that he might take.
Could she but meet again and with him fly—
E'en might she only see him once and die.

But should she bring him harm—that fever taint
Which may be in her veins owns no restraint.
Would she his love and courage thus requite?
With touch of death his youthful beauty blight?
—That beauty aye had gladdened so her sight.
Oh hideous thought! on that she will not dwell,
And yet the horror cannot all repel.
She thinks upon the dead that near her lie,
Recals their sinking wail of agony;
Brings back the morn, seems now so long ago,
When, jubilant with life, and in the glow
Of blithe expectancy, the party gay,
Intent on pleasure, started on their way;
She wanders to the previous bitter past,
The chill neglect that had so long o'ercast
Her days with gloom, and sorrows for the deep
Resentful feeling she had suffered creep
Into her heart—she cannot now atone,
She can but mourn for wrong she may have done.
At such an hour the self-accusing mind

In molehill faults reviewed will mountains find,
And magnify each small remissness in
Affection's service to a grievous sin;
Nor comfort know, save in the fond belief
That those so dear have knowledge of our grief.
But can they know this in those realms of joy
Where Faith is promised bliss without alloy?

&ast;  &ast;  &ast;  &ast;  &ast;  &ast;

At length the daylight fades, and falls the dew,
While o'er the landscape spreads a softened hue.
Familiar birds have ceased their choral song,
And Mavis now, his solo clear and strong
Concluded, shelters 'mid the beechen leaves
Close laced with gossamer the insect weaves.
The crescent moon arises pale and low
And but short time her silver edge will show,
While in the darkling canopy aloft
The stars shine out in growing radiance soft.

Scarce stirs the air, nor breaks with any sound
The deep oppressive stillness reigning round.
She watches with a straining eye and ear
Acute, that must the slightest movement hear ;
There is no sign of what her heart would crave—
His coming—nothing hears she, nothing save
Her own sad sigh of long-suspended breath !
She is alone—alone with sleep and death.


How hard on eager spirits is the strain
When forced in dull inaction to remain.
Man has his share of labour to fulfil—
'Tis Woman's part to suffer and be still.
Against this numb increasing fear she prays,
And with the thought the eye doth upward raise :
It readeth there of worlds around, above ;
Of might illimitable as of love.
Those countless orbs deep mysteries present ;
Labyrinths of skill, to which slight clue is lent.

The mind athirst for knowledge, asks again,
Where is that Heaven we do not seek in vain?
Are those the "many mansions" He hath said
He would prepare for those for whom He bled?
And is our little world the only one
Wherein Redemption's wondrous work was done?
Oh glorious deed! soul-stirring act of Grace!
Eternal gift! What matters where the place?
The Heaven we seek, how long soe'er we roam,
May be within, beyond that radiant dome;
Faith centres it with Him, our God, our Home.
Thus is mortality's too restless sigh
Oft soothed by readings of the quiet sky;
By silent eloquence of tongues on high.


There is a cry—again—and nearer now!
'Tis but the night-jar calling from a bough—
And sinks her heart with disappointed pang,
As out, afar, again those hootings rang.

But now, yes, surely, comes another sound;
A footfall weary on the broken ground
Is drawing near, "Speak, lady, dost thou live?"
"Once more that voice to me doth comfort give!
"Hast Diarmid seen?"  "He comes with loving speed
"Thy rescue to achieve—a daring deed
"Devised with prudence, meriting success."
"May him and thee kind Heaven for ever bless!
"By which way comes he?"  "The long round by sea
"He thought the surest route, altho' there be
"Three points of danger, watchfires, to be passed,
"At risk of life : the flowing tide will last,
"And serve him yet some hours; I go to wait
"His landing.  Soon then hope, should adverse Fate
"Not intervene, that thou may'st be set free,
"And stand beside him on the heathery lea."
He left her.  Softly then some teardrops fell
From the quick-rising and o'erflowing well
Of long-suppressed inquietude of heart.
And will he come—nor ever from her part

Till death dissolve the bond!" Oh grant him true
Through life's long course, so she may never rue
The hour when from these fire-doomed walls she fled,
Which, though her life were numbered with the dead,
Did her unsullied maiden fame protect.
She cannot long on such dark thought reflect,
For comes a tender voice, of love which tells,
And every doubt and every fear dispels.
" Oh Diarmid, brave as true, thou bring'st me life."
" My soul's joy, art thou not my plighted wife?
" To whom but me should'st thou in danger cling?
" Our faithful Iain doth a ladder bring
" Which thou with nerve and caution must descend
" When firm 'tis placed against the turret's bend;
" My boat is waiting in the shallows near,
" To bear us safely from this place of fear."
" And dost thou then not shrink from touch of me?
" I would not harm thee, Diarmid. Set me free
" Upon the grassy sward, I but entreat,
" With power to guide at will my wandering feet;

" The sheltering woods and rocks will me befriend,

" And Providence its sure protection lend.

" I do not fear in freedom thus to wait

" Until the panic, though inordinate,

" Be overpast." " Henceforth I leave thee not,

" And whatsoe'er it be, will share thy lot:

" But for the safety and the just content

" Of those now aiding me, do thou assent

" Unto some prudent measures—I have brought

" Apparel of my sister's, in the thought

" 'Twere better here thou shouldst thy garments leave,

" That thus from them no taint to thee may cleave;

" And for the moment's need, this plaid mayhap

" Within its ample folds will thee enwrap.

" Disrobe thee quick." " Oh Diarmid, must this be ?"

" All risk to shun no other way I see.

" So I beseech thee, do this for my sake."

" For that dear sake I every care will take."

The ladder is adjusted firm—anon

A muffled form sure footing gains thereon

And by the narrow way descends with care,
While those below from speech or sign forbear;
Till love's enfolding arms around her press,
And broken words are heard of tenderness.
Oh throbbing hearts! In what an hour to meet!
What wild triumphant joy! Yes—life *is* sweet.
" Now with all speed betake us to the shore;
" But first our thanks to thee, brave Iain Mòr,
" Are largely due, nor can thy Heaven-blessed aid
" Be but with life long gratitude repaid;
" We leave thee here, for thou hast that to do,
" Will show its mark, while we our flight pursue;
" When troubles well are past, come o'er the brae,
" With lighter heart than when thou didst essay
" Thine arduous task; the Awe will cease to flow
" Ere we forgetfulness of thee can know."
And hurriedly their different ways they seek.
" Now, Mairi, tarry by this sandy creek,
" That here thou may'st in quiet waters bathe
" 'Neath veil of night; this covering plaid unswathe

" And thy fair self from chance of danger free
" By safeguard of ablution cool: and see,
" In passing up I laid on this broad stone
" Thy new habiliments; so now alone
" I leave thee, safe from observation all,
" Though hearing not beyond—when ready, call."
With grateful sense of duty to fulfil—
In newly-felt obedience to his will—
She entering, hides below the rippling waves,
And in their limpid freshness long she laves,
Till sure, if water could all taint remove,
Of hurt to others she must guiltless prove;
Then by the sheltering stone proceeds
Her garments new to don—and little heeds
Their richer stuff, and of their costlier make
Doth in the twilight but small notice take.
On Diarmid soon she calls in timid tones;
Their soft appeal his ear attentive owns,
And coming steps are answering heard apace;
A passing clasp—a hurried fond embrace—

And to the water's edge he hastens on.
That none henceforth the plaid condemned may don,
He ties it firmly round a stone of weight,
And cast into the loch, 'tis left to fate.
To Mairi then returning, on they haste,
And in soft words of re-united love,
The sweets of hope in life recovered, taste.


Ere long they reach the sheltered landing cove;
There signal low upon his horn he blew,
Soon mutely answered by the waiting crew
Who near the boat to the appointed place;
Quick enters the light form with shrouded face,
And Diarmid soon is seated by her side;
Then thrusting off into the broader tide,
Young Hamish speaks, " The dawn will soon be here,
" E'en now, Sir Knight, see where yon streaks appear;
" We dare not venture past the points again,
" All hope discovery to escape were vain;

" But higher up the loch there is an isle
' Where we may sure concealment find awhile ;
" Save for some moss-grown ruins, where of old
" Veiled devotees their beads securely told,
" Of human habitation it is bare,
" Though much with birch and hazel overgrown ;
" And but in quest of sport, none goeth there.
" Within its narrow limits all unknown
" We for a time may hide." " Thou sayest well :
" That haven should we reach ere coming day
" Discover us, and all our work betray.
" The rising song of lark might be the knell
" Of shattered hopes for us, which Heaven forbid,"
Then to the oars they bend, in gloom still hid ;
The minutes pass, with strenuous efforts fraught
Unto the rowers, while in tender thought—
Shown but in furtive pressure of the hand—
In mutual trust the lover's hearts expand.
Now Diarmid sees his oarsmen heed bestow
Upon some object that on shore doth show :

He turns him, and behold, a lurid spot
Which, as he looks, bursts forth in flames upshot.
In strength increasing, brighter yet the glare
Illumines fitfully Maam Callaird's height,
Till far around that red light gleameth there.
" Nay, Mairi, gaze not on such grievous sight,"
But gaze she will, till tears her eyes o'erflow.
Oh what a pang for tender heart—to know
That the still forms of brotherhood and sire
Are fuel for that sure-devouring fire!
No longer from his arm withdraws she, coy,
Her all on Earth, deliverer, guide and joy!
They linger not, though awestruck looks are cast
Upon the raging flame, which hours will last,
And in the annals of that West Countrie
As an event unmatched recorded be.
The gentle spirit quiet sighs doth heave,
As passing on, that haunting scene they leave ;
And eastward turns an anxious troubled eye
Where mountain forms loom clearer 'gainst the sky

As spreads a cold grey light arising thence.
It touches heights, and falls upon the dense
Fir-covered slopes, then on the surface still
Of the dark loch, revealing fear of ill
Depicted in the faces of the crew;
Disquietude that in himself each knew,
Tho' none expressed—their leader too betrays
Uneasy thoughts; his restless searching gaze
Swift wandering round, peers into every nook
As lifts the mist, then turns with tender look
On the slight form Fidelity may claim
As snatched from Death, and rescued in her name.
But rose-tints soft the fleeting grey pursue,
And with the cold light blends a brighter hue.
It shines upon the weary pallid girl,
In languor leaning, all emotion hushed;
Recovered scarce from the bewildering whirl
Of past events, she shows like flower storm-crushed.
Her inborn ease and grace befit right well
The richer garments that new clanship tell;

For Diarmid's tartan she will henceforth wear
And with the fairest of his race compare.
Discarding sorrows with thy robes of yore,
Look up, sweet Mairi: Fate has yet in store
Much good for thee, tho' chequered it may be
With ill, 'tis best that thou canst not foresee.
The present hour is thine—enough to feel
That all thine aching wounds 'twill surely heal;
Enough to know that whatsoe'er betide,
'Twill find thee thus contented at his side;
Enough his hand to touch in clasp so dear;
His voice, still more his whispered words to hear;
Enough his meeting eye—oh joy to see,
Doth turn so oft and lovingly on thee.
Old fears, old doubts are gone, like darkness past;
New life begins with dawn now breaking fast.


At length the lonely, leafy isle they reach—
The wished-for haven gladly hailed by each.

Not this the first time it protection gave
To hapless maid bereaved, who, life to save,
Unto its sacred precincts fled of yore:
Hence "Woman's Isle" the simple name it bore.
They shelter as they can throughout the day,
And with returning night retrace their way
With little risk, for nowhere now is found
The watch so strict; the warning fires around
Have faded in the great funereal blaze
That published wide, with horror and amaze,
The dread catastrophe enacting there.
Light friendly waves the travellers onward bear,
Till up the Awe with flagging strength they wind.
Past doubts new-rising, chill the timid mind,
As landing, Hamish is sent on before,
Their tale to tell and welcome to implore;
And following slow with Mairi, Diarmid tries
To win some smiles of hope, which fear denies.

Their path led by the birch and hazel bank
Where heather, interspersed with grasses dank,
In purple patches grew ; by beechen grove
And avenue, where branching arms above
Met, and commingling, flung luxuriant shade
Upon the space beneath, save where there strayed
Some prying sunbeam through the leafy screen—
Now here, now there, the foliage between,
As breezes light would shift the dancing ray
Which broader fell athwart the turfy way.
It gleamed upon the smooth-barked, stately forms
That passing generations will outlast
Of human hopes; and long will shadows cast
In proud defiance of the western storms,
Though these their symmetry may oft-times mar
By rude destroying force.   In ancient far
Cathedral fane, no aisle than this more grand,
Whereof the architect's is Nature's hand.
Here, then, the pair moved slowly on—each filled
With thoughts their early training had instilled :

The one to stain not his ancestral name,
The other trembling for her maiden fame ;
Both by unselfish true affection stirred,
Regretting that had been so long deferred
Their love's avowal—striving to conceal
Mistrust of answer to their late appeal ;
Through all, impressed by calmness of the scene,
In contrast with the terrors that had been.


Winged Rumour far and wide has noised abroad
The direful facts that food will long afford
For marvel-loving tongues ; and news has come
Of the doomed house and of the ruined home,
But nought of the escape—that still unknown,
Small wonder then discomfiture was shown
At Inverawe, when Hamish did relate
To ears perturbed, the deed heroic done ;
And how that Diarmid did e'en now await
A greeting kind for the poor rescued one.

" Go, tell my son that with him I would speak
" From off the Terrace steps. He must not seek
" To enter here, until such course may seem
" Less hazardous for us than we esteem
" It now to be." The messenger hath sped,
And fear with curiosity is read
In faces round. Yes, they are coming now,
And clears the good old Knight his ruffled brow
As Diarmid leads his shrinking partner on,
Their forms seen moving lithe the sward upon ;
And Clare looks forth with scrutinising eye
Which softens soon in tender sympathy,
And glistens when it meets the anxious glance
That claims from her a sister's countenance.
" Father, much heedless wrong I may have done
" But meanness never—pardon now thy son."
" My son, the brave and faithful merit bear,
" And though I not deny I would mine heir
" Had elsewhere sought than in unfriendly clan
" A helpmeet in our home to dwell—no man

" Shall cast reproach upon thy heart's free choice:
" For Love is wayward, and with dulcet voice,
" In tones unheard maybe 'midst courtly din,
" Doth steal into the citadel within,
" And secret bind with fine magnetic chains
" The conscious will that subjugate remains;
" But if in fault, good reason canst thou plead,
" For in that fair and modest face I read
" All purity and truth.    Daughter, I grieve
" I cannot thee with safety yet receive;
" But in our bothy up Ben-Cruachan's side,
" I pray ye both a brief space to abide,
" Attended but by these devoted few
" Who would, if need were, peril life anew.
" Then, when the panic well is overpast,
" So men no longer look at thee aghast,
" Return : and that no scorn on thee may wait,
" We will entreat, in all befitting state,
" The Church's sanction on thy union fond
" Which now I do pronounce a legal bond;

" Your mutual vows exchanged declaring this.
" Thus, then, the nuptial tie I freely bless,
" Although I can but waft the father's kiss
" I dare not give thee yet.   In happiness,
" Forgetting not the way that thou hast trod,
" As honoured wife and loved, long may'st thou live."
" Oh joy unlooked for and unhoped !   Oh God,
" My coward heart and feeble trust forgive."


So said, so done—and Time went calmly by
Till summons came from Inverawe, to meet
The welcome waiting there.   Thus happily
They left the eagle's haunt, their wild retreat.
Their due espousals then to celebrate,
In pomp assembled all the country side ;
And long the clansmen proudly would relate
How noble Diarmid won his Cameron bride.

K. I. O.

www.ingramcontent.com/pod-product-compliance
Lightning Source LLC
Chambersburg PA
CBHW032203010726
47493CB00008BA/2801